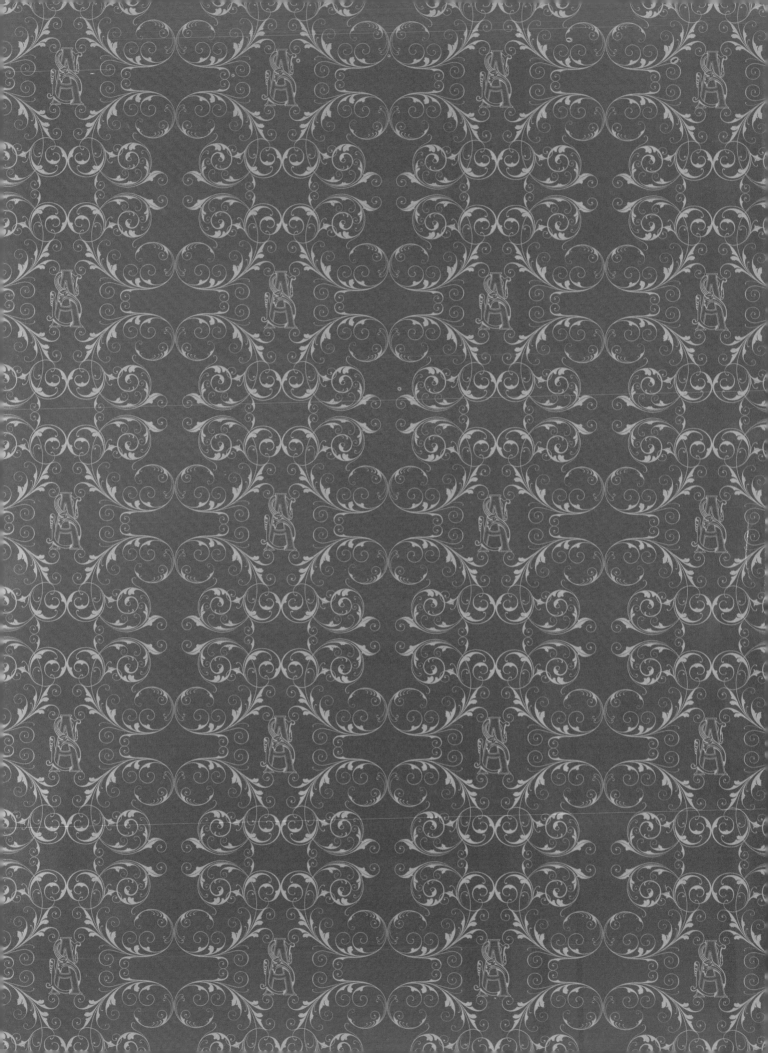

# THE SPIDERWICK CHRONICLES

## THE MOVIE STORYBOOK

adapted by Tracey West
based on the screenplay by Karey Kirkpatrick and David Berenbaum and John Sayles
from the books by Tony DiTerlizzi and Holly Black

SIMON SPOTLIGHT
An imprint of Simon & Schuster Children's Publishing Division
New York   London   Toronto   Sydney
1230 Avenue of the Americas, New York, New York 10020
TM & © 2008 Paramount Pictures. All Rights Reserved.
All rights reserved, including the right of reproduction in whole or in part in any form.
SIMON SPOTLIGHT and colophon are registered trademarks of Simon & Schuster, Inc.
Manufactured in the United States of America
2 4 6 8 10 9 7 5 3 1
ISBN-13: 978-1-4169-5927-4
ISBN-10: 1-4169-5927-0

Jared Grace gazed out the window of the SUV. The moon lit up the big, old house at the end of the driveway.

"What do you think, Jared?" his mom, Helen, asked him.

Jared just sat in silence. He wouldn't even look at her.

Helen got out of the car and headed toward the house. She knew the house wasn't perfect, but she was willing to give it a shot. Even Jared's big sister, Mallory, and his twin brother, Simon, were trying to look on the bright side.

Not Jared.

"Get out of the car," Mallory said, pointing her fencing sword at Jared. "I'm not going to let you keep acting like a jerk," she continued, lunging toward him with her sword.

Trying to dodge her attack, Jared leaped out of the car and grabbed a stick off the ground. "I'll do whatever I want," he said.

It was already dark, and Mallory and Simon started walking toward the house. Jared knew he'd eventually have to go inside, so he began dragging his feet up the driveway. A funny feeling came over him, like he was being watched. He turned around. Was there something in the woods?

Simon was unpacking in their new room when Jared came in.

"Is that our nutty aunt?" Jared asked, pointing to the picture of the family on the wall.

"The guy is Arthur Spiderwick. You know, our great-great-uncle?" Simon explained. "The little girl is the nutty one . . . I mean, Lucinda, his daughter. She used to live here, before they sent her away."

Jared had heard the story. Aunt Lucinda told people that her father was abducted by goblins. Goblins! How ridiculous was that?

After they finished unpacking, Helen started to make dinner. They discovered some pretty strange things in the kitchen cupboard. There were boxes and boxes of oatmeal, lots of salt, and jars filled with honey and tomato sauce.

Strange things were happening in the house too. Helen was missing her car keys. Mallory was missing her fencing medal. And Jared was getting blamed for everything.

"I didn't take the stupid medal!" Jared protested.

Later on Jared started hearing a skittering sound inside the walls.

"Probably a red squirrel," Simon said.

Jared started tapping the wall with a broom, trying to follow the creature's movements. After convincing Mallory and Simon that it wasn't a red squirrel, they helped him search. Finally, Jared pulled a huge chunk of plaster off the wall to reveal an old dumbwaiter. It was filled with lots of little things, from coins to dollhouse furniture.

"Hey, there are Mom's keys!" Mallory cried. "And my medal!"

She gave Jared a fierce stare.

"You think I took it and hid it here?" Jared cried.

Jared was going to find out what was really going on. Later he climbed inside the dumbwaiter. He pulled himself up to the top of the house. The dumbwaiter's last stop was a secret room—Arthur Spiderwick's study!

While exploring the dusty old study, Jared found a very old leather-bound book. A wax seal held the cover shut. Jared read the note on the cover.

*Warning!*

*Do not dare to read this book. For if you take one fateful look,*
*you barter at your life's expense—and face a deadly consequence.*

Ignoring the warning, Jared picked up the book. As if by magic, a message appeared in the dust on top of the old desk.

*Jared Grace, leave this place.*

Jared knew he was not alone. He took the book back to his room. While Simon slept, Jared broke the wax seal, opened *Arthur Spiderwick's Field Guide to the Fantastical World Around You*, and began to read. . . .

The pages were filled with drawings and descriptions of creatures that Jared had never seen or heard of in his life. But Arthur Spiderwick could see all kinds of fantastical creatures with a thing he called the Seeing Stone, and he recorded all of his findings in this book. The book was filled with information about sprites, pixies, phookas, goblins, and other creatures.

Strange things happened while Jared was reading. Something opened the latch on the cage holding Simon's mice. Jared heard an eerie howl in the woods. He thought he saw something small run across his room.

But Jared kept reading. He was very interested in reading about a creature called a house brownie. Arthur Spiderwick said that brownies guarded the houses where they lived. When brownies got angry, they turned into boggarts. Boggarts could cause a lot of trouble.

Then Jared heard a loud scream. It was Mallory!

Jared and Simon ran to Mallory's room. Her long hair was tied to the headboard of her bed! Once again she blamed Jared.

After untangling Mallory, the boys went back to their room. Jared showed Simon the book and pointed to the picture of a brownie named Thimbletack.

"This is what was living in the dumbwaiter," Jared said. "I think it wants us to leave the house."

Simon wasn't sure what to believe. But he was pretty sure nobody would believe Jared.

The next day Jared read more about the brownie. He had a feeling that Thimbletack the brownie had turned into a boggart. The book said a boggart had to be "appeased" to turn back into a brownie. Jared told Simon and Mallory what he had found.

"'Appease'" means to make nice," Simon explained.

"It likes honey," Jared said, and he suddenly realized something. "That's why all that honey's in the kitchen."

Mallory didn't believe him. "Don't fall for this, Simon," she warned.

Then a loud yell came from inside the house.

"Jared Grace! Get in here!"

The kitchen was a huge mess. Food was splattered everywhere. Helen was sure Jared had done it because he was angry about the move.

But Jared knew the truth. Thimbletack the boggart wanted them out of the house. He would keep causing trouble until he was appeased.

Jared needed a plan—fast.

The next morning Jared took a birdhouse from one of the trees outside. He put some new shiny things inside to replace the ones they had taken from the dumbwaiter. Then he took the birdhouse up to the secret study. He put it on a table and set a jar of honey and some crackers next to it.

"Um, sorry we wrecked your home," Jared said out loud. "But I've made you a new one. We really are sorry. Maybe you could give Simon's mice back."

Jared sat down. He waited and waited. Then he drifted off to sleep. The tickling of mouse whiskers woke him up. The mice were back!

Then Jared heard a singsong voice behind the birdhouse.

*The honey's sweet, the brownie pleased.*

*And Thimbletack is now appeased.*

A tiny little creature with pointy ears was happily eating the honey. Jared was scared at first. But Thimbletack was friendly, even though he seemed upset.

"I have failed, failed, failed!" he wailed. "One simple, simple task. Protect the book. Protect the book. Keep it in the circle."

Jared knew that Arthur Spiderwick had asked Thimbletack to keep the book safe. He had read all about the protective toadstool circle that surrounded the house in Arthur's book.

"So the protective circle protects the house . . . to protect the book. Protect it from who?" he asked Thimbletack.

Jared looked out the window at the mushrooms. Simon was walking out of the circle, toward the woods. Suddenly Simon screamed. Something was pulling him into the woods!

"You've unleashed them. They're coming!" cried Thimbletack. "The goblins and the ogre, the lord of them! Go ahead, have a look at the mess you've made!"

With that, Thimbletack tossed Jared the Seeing Stone. Jared looked through it. A gang of ugly goblins had grabbed Simon!

Jared grabbed the book and dashed out of the house and into the woods. The goblins had trapped Simon in a cage. Jared watched, hidden in the trees until—*crunch!* A chubby hobgoblin broke the silence, chomping down on a small yellow bird. Jared looked up and saw that the creature was trapped in a cage.

"I am Hogsqueal. And I am here on a mission: to destroy the ogre, Mulgarath, who killed my family! You can free me from this cage!"

"Will you help me save my brother?" Jared asked.

"Yes! We are allies now!" Hogsqueal answered. "Now drop the stone. You'll need both hands to fight a goblin."

"But I can't see them without—"

With that, Hogsqueal spit in Jared's eyes!

"I have given you the Sight," Hosqueal proclaimed, "a gift that only a hobgoblin can bestow."

His eyes were blurry at first, but when Jared wiped away the spit, he could see Hogsqueal without using the Seeing Stone.

Suddenly the goblins began to chant, "Mul-ga-rath! Mul-ga-rath!"

A wrinkled old man appeared. It was Mulgarath, the ogre. He demanded that Simon give him Arthur Spiderwick's book.

"I don't have it," Simon said. "But I know where it is. Let me go and I'll get it for you."

Mulgarath agreed. "If you fail, my friends will become very . . . aggravated," he warned.

Simon ran away as fast as he could. Jared turned to follow him, but he got tangled in a branch. Down below, Mulgarath began to transform. He changed from a skinny old man to a huge, ugly monster!

He turned to face the goblin leader. "Redcap, follow him. Wait for him to give you the book," Mulgarath growled. "Then kill them. Kill them all!"

Jared caught up with Simon and warned him about what the ogre had said. Simon was angry with Jared for causing all of this. He grabbed the book from Jared, but in the struggle it fell to the ground.

"BOOOOOK!" yelled Redcap as swarms of goblins began closing in.

Grabbing the book, Jared and Simon ran for the circle. Jared knew they would be safe there. But when they reached the house, Mallory was outside. They tried to explain to her what was going on, but she didn't believe them.

Suddenly the goblins started attacking her! Jared gave her the Seeing Stone, and sure enough, she saw swarms of ugly goblins all around. She began fighting them off with her fencing sword.

Finally, they all made it into the house. They were safe inside the circle—for now.

An army of goblins surrounded the house. They waited right outside the circle of toadstools. Mulgarath showed up too.

"What are those things? What do they want?" Mallory asked.

"They want the book," Jared explained.

"Then just give it to them!" she said angrily.

"NO!" cried a voice. "Goblins must not have the book. All will die! All will die!" Thimbletack had just appeared out of thin air.

"AHHH!" screamed Mallory and Simon together. "What *is* that thing?" Mallory cried.

"It's okay," explained Jared. "Just don't make him angry."

Everyone took a deep breath and tried to calm down while Thimbletack explained that the book held many secrets. If Mulgarath got hold of the secrets, the world would be in great danger.

They decided to try to destroy the book so no one could have it. So they took it outside and Jared set it on fire. Mulgarath was furious, but he could not step inside the protective circle. The flames burned high—but nothing happened to the book! Soon the kids realized that Arthur Spiderwick must have used a charm to protect it from all harm.

Jared knew there had to be a way to destroy the book, so he came up with a new plan. "We have to go see Aunt Lucinda. She lived here, and it's her father's book. She can tell us what to do."

So Jared and Mallory decided to go see her—but she was in a hospital in town. Simon stayed home, but he gave Mallory an eyepiece he found in Arthur's study. The Seeing Stone fit right inside. Now Mallory could still use both of her hands.

Thimbletack knew a secret way into town. After watching Jared lock the book safely in its chest, Thumbletack helped the kids escape.

While Simon distracted the goblins, Jared and Mallory ran out of the toadstool circle into the woods. The goblins chased them, but they made it to the secret tunnel just in time.

As Jared and Mallory raced through the tunnel, they began to hear the thundering of footsteps and the hissing sound of something breathing heavily.

"That doesn't sound good!" Mallory cried.

It was a mole troll. The hideous creature barreled after them with a hungry look in its eye; it had been sent by the goblins. Finally, the kids exited the tunnel. They climbed up through a manhole cover and onto the street, with the troll grunting at their heels when—*splat!* A passing truck smashed into the beast, allowing the kids to escape. They dashed down the street to Woodhaven Hospital.

"She'll be excited to have visitors," the nurse said with a smile.

Aunt Lucinda was sitting outside, surrounded by pretty little sprites. Of course, the nurses couldn't see them, but Jared and Mallory could. Aunt Lucinda was so happy to see Jared and Mallory, but her mood changed once she saw that Jared had brought the book with him. He had tricked Thimbletack and everyone else, locking Mallory's diary in the chest instead.

"Inside. Quickly," Aunt Lucinda said, motioning for the kids to move indoors. "This book has brought nothing but misery to my family," she said. Her eyes filled with tears as she remembered the last day she saw her father. Mulgarath had found out about the book, and he wanted it more than anything. So he ordered the goblins to grab Arthur, and Lucinda never saw him again.

"The sprites say my father is alive," Aunt Lucinda said. "You must find him, bring him this book, and have him destroy it. It is your only hope."

Just then Redcap came crashing through the window! He clawed at the book, tearing off a few pages. Aunt Lucinda quickly grabbed some salt from the circle she always kept surrounding her bed and threw a handful in Redcap's face. He shrieked and ran away.

At that moment their mother showed up at the hospital—and she was furious! Having spotted her kids running through town, she left her first day of work early to follow them. She was angry and confused. In the car Jared told her all about the book and the ogre; even Mallory backed him up. But Helen didn't believe any of it.

"Do you think I don't see what's going on here? You hate the house and you want to go back to New York. But that's not going to happen," Helen told them as she pulled up to the house. After dropping them off, she went back to work.

Jared and Mallory returned to find Simon in the kitchen, filling bags with a combination of goblin defenses: tomato sauce, salt, and oatmeal—all the things that goblins hate.

While the kids were planning their next move, Redcap brought Mulgarath the pages of the book he had managed to steal. The ogre read them carefully. Though he was angry that he didn't have the whole book, he was pleasantly surprised to learn how to break the spell of the protective circle.

"When the moon rises, the book will be mine!" he howled.

Luckily, Hogsqueal was watching from a tree branch. He swallowed the rest of the juicy bird he was eating and ran straight to the house to warn Jared of Mulgarath's plan. Hogsqueal gave both Mallory and Simon the Sight, then ran outside, where dozens of birdhouses dangled from the trees.

They had to act quickly. Once the moon rose, Mulgarath and the goblins would enter the circle, take the book—and kill them all!

Jared thought he knew how to find Arthur Spiderwick. In the guide he had come across a creature that was Arthur's loyal companion, a griffin. He summoned the griffin with the special call he had read about in the book. Arthur's companion arrived, and the kids climbed on the griffin's back and flew off to a hidden glade between the mountains.

Aunt Lucinda was right. Arthur Spiderwick was alive, surrounded by thousands of tiny creatures called sylphs who made him forget how much time had passed and kept him enchanted with their magical singing.

"I can't help you," Arthur told Jared. "You read the book. You have the knowledge. Use it to stop Mulgarath."

Jared was disappointed, but there was nothing else he could do. The griffin flew them back to the house just as the moon was rising. Helen was back home, and she was angrier than ever.

Then Jared gave her the Seeing Stone. She looked through the Stone and saw Mulgarath and the goblins getting ready to attack.

"We have to protect the house. Understand?" Jared said.

Helen finally believed him, and nodded in agreement. The family went to work. They poured salt on the windowsills. They made more tomato sauce goblin bombs. They prepared to protect their home.

Then . . . *bam! Bam! Bam!* The goblins slammed into the windows. They slammed into the doors. But they couldn't get in.

But the goblins wouldn't give up. They broke through the roof, pushed holes through the basement, and broke through the ceiling. Jared hurled goblin defenses at them at lightning speed. Mallory sprayed them with saltwater. But the goblins kept coming.

The family barricaded themselves in the kitchen.

"What do we do?" Jared wailed. "This won't hold for long!"

Simon looked at all the jars of tomato sauce. He looked at the oven.

He had an idea. . . .

*Slam!* Moments later Mulgarath and the goblins broke through the kitchen door. But Jared and his family were nowhere in sight.

*Boom!* The oven exploded, shooting tomato sauce all over the kitchen. The goblins screamed as the sauce covered them, scorching their skin.

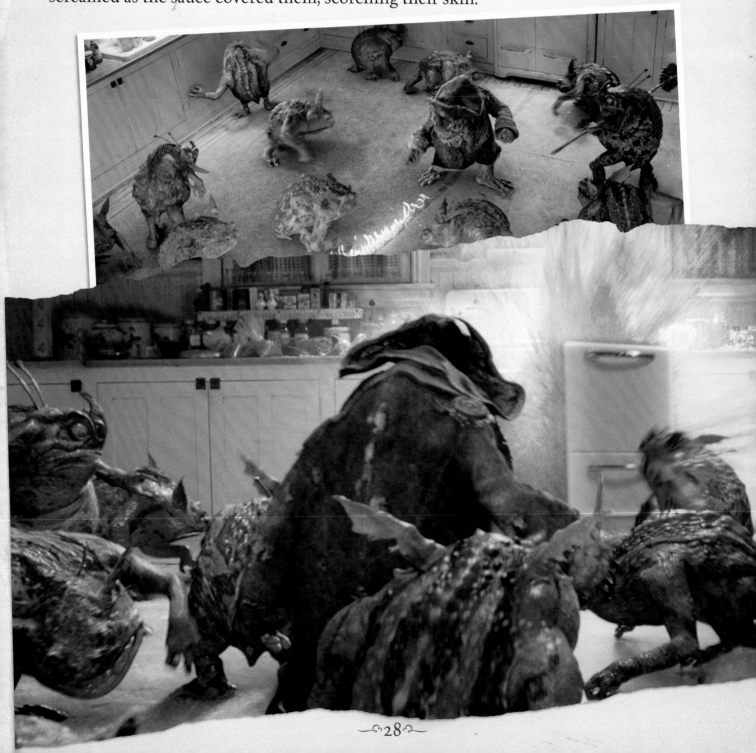

Then, all of a sudden, everything got quiet. Jared and his family crawled out of their hiding places. Jared still held the book tightly.

"Book safe?" Thimbletack asked.

"Book safe," said Jared, smiling.

But the fight was not over yet. The tomato sauce had not stopped Mulgarath.

"Give me the book!" he bellowed.

Jared jumped into the dumbwaiter. He pulled himself up to the secret study. Mulgarath transformed into a snake and slithered his way up through the wall after Jared.

Jared continued to climb up through the house until he escaped onto the roof. Mulgarath transformed back into his ogre form and burst through the roof. He swiped at Jared, trying to grab the book. There was nowhere else for Jared to go. He was trapped.

"Give me that book!" Mulgarath roared, climbing closer and closer.

Jared looked around. Below him were groves of trees and birdhouses. He could see Hogsqueal in one of the houses, munching on a bird.

Then Jared had a thought. Mulgarath could transform into any form he wanted. Just maybe . . .

"You want the book? Go get it!" Jared yelled, and he tossed the book off the roof, toward the trees where the birdhouses sat.

With a cry, Mulgarath transformed into a crow and zoomed after the book, hoping to catch it. He extended his sharp talons . . . and—*crunch*!

Hogsqueal reached out and grabbed the crow. He ate Mulgarath in one gulp!

Hogsqueal burped. "Oooh. That one was nasty!"

The book was finally safe! "Hogsqueal," cried Jared, "you did it! You killed Mulgarath!"

"The taste of vengeance is sweet! I can still taste it a little," Hogsqueal cheered, licking his fingers clean.

With the goblins gone, the family brought Aunt Lucinda back to the house. She didn't end up staying long. The sylphs brought Arthur back to see his daughter, and she decided to go back to the glade with her father.

Jared smiled. Living in the Spiderwick house didn't seem so horrible anymore. After all, there was a fantastical world just waiting to be explored!